E
H123o

Out of the Nursery, Into the Night

Out of the Nursery, Into the Night

By Kathleen Hague · Illustrated by Michael Hague

Henry Holt and Company
New York

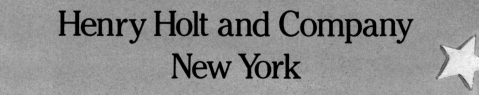

Library of Congress Cataloging in Publication Data
Hague, Kathleen.
Out of the nursery, into the night.
Summary: Describes in rhymed text and illustrations
some of the wonderful dreams dreamed by a group of
teddy bears during the night.
[1. Teddy bears—Fiction.   2. Dreams—Fiction.
3. Stories in rhyme]   I. Hague, Michael, ill.
II. Title.
PZ8.3.H11930u   1986   [E]   86-14270
ISBN: 0-8050-0088-7
Designed by Marc Cheshire
First Edition Printed in the United States of America
1 3 5 7 9 10 8 6 4 2

ISBN 0-8050-0088-7

With love to Dordor

K.H. & M.H.

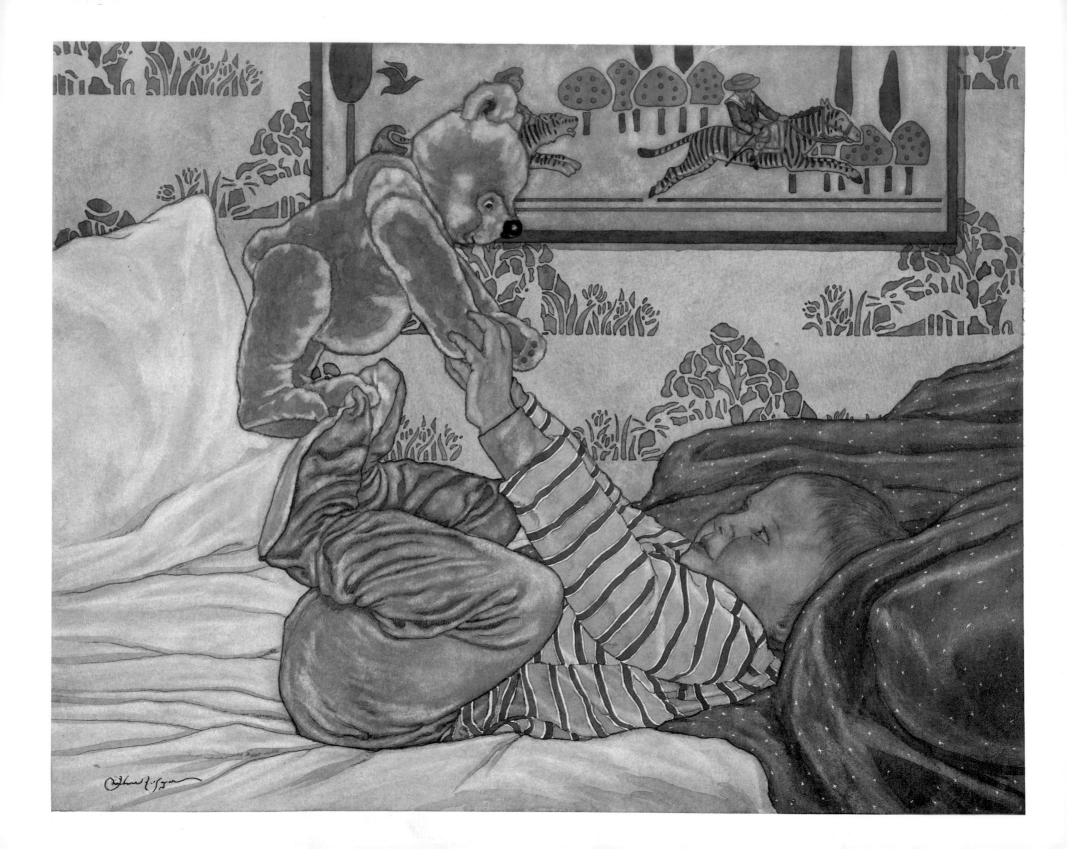

When the daytime light is all but gone
And you're lying in your bed;
When the nighttime tuck-me-ins are done
And all your prayers are said;
When it seems you cannot fall asleep
And your playing's not quite done;
Do like these sleepy little bears,
And dream yourself some fun.

Fairies take Max on a dream flight,
Out of the nursery, into the night.
Chasing the stars to and fro,
While night lights watch from far below.

Scotty dreams of a triceratops.
He rides the beast on tippy-tops.
Through the town they walk along,
While Scotty sings a silly song.

This is the dream of Peggy Sue.
She is a rowdy buckaroo.
On her bronc she roams the sky,
Roping comets straying by.

Chris is a knight known far and wide.
Across dream kingdoms he will ride.
Righting wrongs that have been done,
And taming dragons—every one.

To Edward all his dream's a stage.
At the circus he is the rage.
Large crowds come from all around.
To see the world's best juggling clown.

Kimberly goes to the penguin coast,
Her pockets stuffed with bits of toast.
Feathered friends greet her each night,
And hungrily they eat each bite.

Ann swims through her dream in the sea.
A fin is where her feet should be.
A treasure hunt's what she likes best,
For pieces of eight in a treasure chest.

Each night in his sleep David knows
That in his room a toyland grows.
In this dream there isn't a tear,
For only giggles are spoken here.

Bess sees a monster in her dreams.
It's not as scary as it seems.
She made him up in her head,
And now he stands guard by her bed.

Ruth explores an enchanted place,
A look of wonder on her face.
A children's moon hangs in the sky
While she listens to Pan's lullaby

In Arthur's dream he casts a spell;
Abracadabra works quite well.
To brighten up the midnight skies,
He conjures up some butterflies.

Heather dreamed she was on a hunt
To catch the flying elephant.
She used honey as her bait,
And hadn't very long to wait.

The teddy bears have shared their dreams,
And these are but a few;
So now it's time to close your eyes,
And dream a dream for you.